Curse of the Pharaoh's Daughter

Michelle Hartman

Table of contents

Chapter 1

The Royal Prophecy

The sun hung high in the azure sky, casting its golden rays over the sprawling palace of Thebes. The palace's grandeur stood unmatched, with its tall columns and carved statues serving as a testament to the might of Pharaoh Ramses. Inside, the air buzzed with anticipation as the court prepared for the grand celebration honoring the Pharaoh's reign.

Princess Neferet, daughter of Pharaoh Ramses, watched the preparations from her balcony. Her dark eyes, filled with curiosity and intelligence, scanned the bustling courtyard below. The servants hurried back and forth, arranging flowers, preparing lavish dishes, and hanging colorful banners. Neferet's heart swelled with pride at the sight of her father's thriving kingdom.

"Neferet," a voice called from behind. She turned to see her father, Pharaoh Ramses, approaching with a warm smile. His regal presence commanded respect, yet his eyes softened whenever he looked at his daughter.

"Father," Neferet greeted, bowing her head.

"Are you ready for the celebration?" Ramses asked, placing a hand on her shoulder.

"Yes, Father. The palace looks magnificent," Neferet replied, her smile mirroring his.

As the sun set, casting a golden hue over the palace, the royal family gathered in the grand hall. Musicians played enchanting melodies on their lyres and harps, and dancers moved with their movements, telling stories of ancient gods and heroic deeds. Nobles, all dressed in their finest attire, filled the hall with their laughter and chatter.

Amid the revelry, a hush fell over the crowd as a mysterious figure entered the hall. The seer, draped in dark robes and adorned with strange amulets, moved with an air of wisdom. His eyes, deep and unfathomable, seemed to pierce through the very soul of those he looked upon.

Pharaoh Ramses raised a hand, signaling for silence. "Welcome, seer. Your presence that honors us."

The seer bowed. "Pharaoh Ramses, I come bearing a prophecy, one that speaks of great peril and hope for your lineage."

A murmur spread through the crowd, but the Pharaoh's stern gaze silenced it. "Speak your prophecy, wise one."

The seer stepped forward, his voice echoing through the hall. "In the shadows of time, a curse lies dormant, tied to the blood of the Pharaohs. It whispers of ancient evils and forgotten sorrows. When the stars align, the curse shall awaken, bringing forth a darkness that threatens to consume the land."

Gasps of fear and confusion rippled through the crowd. Neferet's heart pounded in her chest as she listened, her mind racing with questions.

The seer continued, "But there is hope. The true heir, brave and wise, shall rise to face the darkness. They will uncover the secrets of the past and wield the power to break the curse. Their courage and resolve can only save the kingdom."

The seer's words hung heavy in the air, and a palpable tension settled over the hall. Neferet glanced at her father, who stood silent and thoughtful, his eyes fixed on the seer.

"Thank you, seer," Pharaoh Ramses finally said, his voice steady. "We shall heed your warning and prepare for what may come."

As the seer bowed and took his leave, the celebration resumed, but the mood had shifted. The nobles whispered amongst themselves, speculating about the prophecy and its implications. Neferet, however, felt a strange determination stirring within her.

Later that night, as the moon bathed the palace in its silvery light, Neferet sat in her chamber, unable to shake the seer's words from her mind. The prophecy spoke of a curse and a true heir. Could it be referring to her? She had always felt a deep connection to the history and legends of her ancestors, a curiosity that often led her to explore the hidden corners of the palace.

"Princess Neferet," a soft voice called from the doorway. It was Amara, her loyal servant and childhood friend. "Are you alright?"

Neferet smiled at Amara, grateful for her comforting presence. "I'm fine, Amara. Just thinking about the prophecy."

Amara nodded, her eyes reflecting the same concern. "It was indeed unsettling. But in you, Neferet. You have always been strong and brave."

Neferet sighed, leaning back against her cushions. "Thank you, Amara. I wish I knew more about this curse and how to stop it."

Amara hesitated, then spoke in a hushed tone. "There are stories, ancient tales, about a hidden chamber in the palace. It is said to hold secrets from the time of the first Pharaohs."

Neferet's eyes widened with interest. "A hidden chamber? Where?"

Amara shrugged. "I don't know exactly. But if anyone can find it, it's you, Neferet."

Determined, Neferet decided. She'd find this hidden chamber and uncover the secrets it held. If the prophecy proved true, she would need to be ready to confront any darkness that lay ahead.

As the palace slept, Neferet's mind buzzed with plans and possibilities. She wouldn't rest until she had the answers she sought. Little did she know, her journey was only beginning, and the fate of the kingdom rested on her shoulders.

Chapter 2

A Forbidden Discovery

The early morning sun cast long shadows across the palace corridors as Neferet moved through the hallways. Her heart raced with anticipation and a hint of apprehension. She had begun her search for the hidden chamber, convinced that the secrets it held were crucial to understanding the prophecy.

Neferet made her way to the library, a vast room filled with scrolls and tablets containing the wisdom of ages. She had spent countless hours here as a child, fascinated by the stories and knowledge within. Today, she sought something more specific—clues to the hidden chamber.

She approached the head scribe, Paser, a wise and elderly man who had served her family for decades. "Good morning, Paser," she greeted him.

"Good morning, Princess Neferet," Paser replied, his eyes twinkling with curiosity. "What brings you to the library so early?"

"I seek your guidance, Paser. There is something I need to find—an ancient chamber hidden within the palace. Do you know anything about it?"

Paser's expression grew serious. "The hidden chamber, you say? People believe the tomb contains secrets from the time of the first Pharaohs, secrets that were supposed to be forgotten."

Neferet nodded. "Yes, it holds the key to understanding the prophecy and the curse. Please, Paser, help me find it."

Paser sighed, then gestured for her to follow. He took her to a secluded corner of the library, where they kept ancient maps and blueprints of the palace. "These are the oldest records we have," he explained. "If there is a hidden chamber, this text might mention it."

Together, they pored over the maps, searching for any sign of a concealed room or passageway. After hours of meticulous examination, Neferet's eyes landed on a faint marking that seemed out of place.

"Look here," she said, pointing to the mark. "This symbol—it's different from the others."

Paser leaned in, adjusting his spectacles. "Ah, yes. That symbol represents a secret passage. For centuries, a sealed-off part of the palace leads to it."

Neferet's heart skipped a beat. "This must be it. Thank you, Paser."

Determined to uncover the secrets of the hidden chamber, Neferet made her way to the location showed on the map. A tapestry depicting the gods of old hid the passage. She moved the tapestry aside, revealing a narrow, dusty corridor.

Torch in hand, Neferet ventured into the passage, the air growing cooler and mustier as she descended. Ancient hieroglyphs lined the walls, their meanings lost to time. After what felt like an eternity, she reached a heavy stone door adorned with intricate carvings.

With a deep breath, Neferet pushed the door open. It creaked and groaned, finally giving way to reveal a lit chamber filled with relics and scrolls. The air was thick with the scent of old parchment and incense.

Neferet stepped inside, her eyes wide with wonder. The chamber was a treasure trove of ancient knowledge. Shelves lined the walls, filled with scrolls that seemed to pulse with the weight of centuries. In the center of the room stood a large stone pedestal upon which rested a golden amulet.

She approached the pedestal, her fingers brushing the surface of the amulet. Symbols crafted seemed to shimmer in the torchlight. Neferet's gaze focused on a scroll lying next to the amulet. Carefully, she unrolled it, revealing a detailed account of the curse.

The scroll told the story of Seti, a powerful sorcerer who had once served the Pharaoh. Seti's ambition and dark magic had led him to seek immortality, but his actions had brought great suffering to the kingdom. To stop him, the Pharaoh's ancestors had cursed and entombed him, hoping to bury his evil forever.

Neferet's mind raced as she absorbed the information. The curse indeed tied her to her bloodline, and she had to stop it. She knew now that the amulet held the key to breaking the curse.

As she pondered her next move, a soft rustling sound caught her attention. She turned to see a shadowy figure lurking in the doorway. Her heart pounded as she realized she was not alone.

"Who's there?" she called out, her voice echoing in the chamber.

The figure stepped forward, revealing a familiar face. It was Anen, the high priest.

"Princess Neferet," he said, his voice calm and authoritative. "I had a feeling you might come here."

"Anen," Neferet breathed a sigh of relief. "I found the chamber and the amulet. It's true—the curse is real."

Anen nodded. "Yes, and it is imperative that we handle this with the utmost care. The amulet holds power, but you must use it to break the curse."

Neferet looked at him, determination in her eyes. "I will do whatever it takes to save our kingdom. What must I do?"

Anen smiled, placing a reassuring hand on her shoulder. "First, we must gather the knowledge and allies. This is not a task you can undertake alone."

Neferet nodded, her resolve strengthening. She had taken the first step in her quest, and with Anen's guidance, she felt ready to face whatever challenges lay ahead.

As they left the hidden chamber, Neferet's mind was already racing with plans. She knew her journey had only begun, and the fate of her kingdom depended on her success. With the amulet in hand and the ancient knowledge she had uncovered, she felt a glimmer of hope.

Neferet, along with Anen and the allies she would gather, determined to break the curse and restore peace to her land. Little did she know the true extent of the challenges and dangers that awaited her.

Chapter 3

Whispers in the Tomb

The moon hung low in the sky, casting a silvery glow over the palace grounds as Neferet and Amara slipped through the shadows. The revelation of the cursed mummy had set Neferet's mind racing, and she knew she had to uncover more about Seti and the curse that bound him. With the amulet tucked into her robes, Neferet led the way toward the ancient tomb mentioned in the scrolls.

Amara, ever loyal and brave, kept close to Neferet's side. "Are you sure about this, Neferet?" she whispered, her eyes darting around them.

"We have to know more," Neferet replied. "The answers are in that tomb. We can't afford to wait any longer."

The tomb lay beyond the palace walls, in a secluded area rarely visited by anyone. Legends and fear surrounded the place, with tales of it being cursed and guarded by ancient spirits. As they approached, the air grew cooler, and an eerie silence settled around them.

A grand, weathered archway adorned with hieroglyphs marked the entrance to the tomb, glowing in the moonlight. Neferet paused for a moment, taking a deep breath before stepping inside. The passageway was narrow and dark, the only light coming from the torches they carried.

As they ventured deeper into the tomb, they encountered mustier air and intricate carvings lining the walls depicting scenes of ancient rituals and battles. Whispers seemed to echo around them, faint and indistinct, as if the very walls were speaking.

"Do you hear that?" Amara asked, her voice trembling.

Neferet nodded. "Yes, it's as if the tomb is alive with the voices of the past."

They reached a large chamber, its ceiling supported by towering columns. At the center stood a massive stone sarcophagus, its surface covered in more hieroglyphs and symbols. Neferet's heart pounded as she approached the sarcophagus, feeling the weight of history and destiny pressing down on her.

"This must be Seti's resting place," Neferet said, her voice above a whisper.

As she examined the sarcophagus, she noticed a series of symbols that matched those on the amulet. Carefully, she placed the amulet into a recess on the sarcophagus, and with a deep, rumbling sound, the lid shifted.

Suddenly, the whispers grew louder, forming coherent words. "Beware, those who dare to disturb the eternal rest of Seti," the voices intoned. "The curse will awaken, and darkness shall reign."

Neferet and Amara exchanged a nervous glance but pressed on. The lid of the sarcophagus slid open, revealing the mummified remains of Seti. The surrounding air seemed to grow colder, and a dark presence filled the chamber.

"Neferet, we must be careful," Amara warned, her eyes wide with fear.

Neferet nodded, her gaze fixed on the mummy. "I know, Amara. But we need to understand what we're dealing with."

Among the items inside the sarcophagus, Neferet found a scroll, its papyrus brittle with age. She carefully unrolled it, revealing more details about the curse and Seti's dark powers. The scroll spoke of a ritual that could bind Seti's spirit and prevent him from wreaking havoc, but it required powerful artifacts and knowledge of ancient magic.

As she read, the whispers intensified, and a ghostly figure materialized above the sarcophagus. It was Seti, his spectral form radiating malevolent energy. His eyes, glowing with an unnatural light, fixed on Neferet.

"You dare to disturb my slumber? "Seti's voice echoed through the chamber, filled with anger and contempt. "You will never lift the curse upon your bloodline." I will reclaim my power and plunge this land into darkness."

Neferet stood her ground, clutching the amulet tightly. "I will stop you, Seti. I will break the curse and protect my people."

Seti's laughter was a chilling sound. "Foolish child. You do not know the forces you are dealing with. The curse is eternal, and my power is boundless."

With that, Seti's spectral form vanished, and the chamber grew silent once more. The weight of their task pressed heavily upon Neferet and Amara as they stood in the dim light.

"We need to leave now," Amara urged, pulling Neferet towards the exit.

Neferet nodded, but her mind was already racing with plans. The scroll had provided crucial information, and she knew they had to act quickly to gather the artifacts and knowledge needed to perform the ritual.

As they made their way back to the palace, Neferet felt a renewed sense of purpose. The encounter with Seti had only strengthened her resolve. She would not rest until she broke the curse and ensured the safety of her kingdom.

Upon their return, Neferet sought Anen, the high priest, and shared everything they had discovered. Anen listened intently, his expression grave.

Anen declared, "This is indeed serious."He stated preparations must begin immediately. The ritual requires not only the artifacts but also great wisdom and strength of will."

Neferet nodded. "I will do whatever it takes. We must gather the knowledge and allies. There is no time to waste."

Anen placed a reassuring hand on her shoulder. "You have the heart of a true leader, Neferet. Together, we will overcome this darkness."

With Anen's guidance, Neferet planned the next steps of their journey. They would need to travel to distant lands, face unknown dangers, and seek powerful allies. The road ahead would be long and treacherous, but Neferet was ready. She had taken the first steps towards breaking the curse and would not stop until she had ensured the safety of her people and banished the darkness forever.

Chapter 4

The Awakening of the Cursed Mummy

The first light of dawn filtered through the palace windows as Neferet sat with Anen, Paser, and Amara in the royal chamber. The ancient scroll lay open on the table before them, its cryptic words and symbols a testament to the dark history they faced.

"The scroll mentions several powerful artifacts needed for the ritual," Neferet explained, tracing her finger over the delicate papyrus. "We have the amulet, but we need to find the remaining items."

Anen nodded thoughtfully. "Yes, but we must act quickly. The encounter with Seti has likely set events into motion. We cannot afford to delay."

As they discussed their plans, a commotion erupted outside the chamber. The doors burst open, and a guard rushed in, his face pale with fear.

"Your Highness, the village near the palace... it's under attack. A strange, dark force has appeared, and people are being struck down by an unknown plague."

Neferet's heart raced. "Seti. He's already started to unleash the curse."

Without hesitation, Neferet rose to her feet. "We must go to the village and help them. Anen, gather the priests. Paser, prepare whatever medicinal supplies we have. Amara, come with me."

As they hurried to the village, Neferet's mind churned with thoughts of the ancient curse and the suffering it was causing. She knew they had to act swiftly to contain the damage and stop Seti.

The village was in chaos when they arrived. People lay stricken with illness, their faces contorted in pain. Dark clouds loomed overhead, casting an eerie pall over the scene. The air was thick with fear and despair.

Neferet knelt beside an elderly woman, her breathing shallow and labored. "We will help you," she promised, her voice steady despite the turmoil around her.

Anen and the priests performed cleansing rituals, their chants filling the air with a sense of urgency. Paser and the other healers tended to the sick, using all the knowledge and resources at their disposal to ease their suffering.

As Neferet moved through the village, she felt a dark presence watching her. She turned to see a figure shrouded in shadows, its eyes glowing with malevolent light. It was Seti, his spectral form radiating an aura of pure evil.

"You cannot save them," Seti's voice echoed through her mind. "The curse is unstoppable. Your efforts are futile."

Neferet's resolve hardened. "I will not let you destroy my people, Seti. I will stop you."

Seti's laughter was a chilling sound. "You are but a child, playing with forces beyond your understanding. The curse will consume everything you hold dear."

With a wave of his hand, Seti unleashed a wave of dark energy that spread through the village, intensifying the plague and causing further suffering. Neferet felt a surge of anger and determination. She knew she had to find the remaining artifacts and perform the ritual before it was too late.

Back at the palace, Neferet gathered her allies in the grand hall. The mood was somber, but there was a shared sense of purpose.

"We must find the remaining artifacts mentioned in the scroll," Neferet said, her voice firm. "The Scepter of Ra, the Sacred Lotus, and the Eye of Horus. They are our only hope of breaking the curse and stopping Seti."

Anen stepped forward, his expression serious. "Many believe that the Temple of Karnak hides the Scepter of Ra. Rumors suggest that the nomadic tribe in the eastern desert has the Eye of Horus and the Sacred Lotus blooms in the Valley of the Kings."

"We will split into teams," Neferet continued. "Anen and Paser, you will go to Karnak. Amara and I will search for the Sacred Lotus. Khepri, our warrior ally, will lead a team to find the nomadic tribe and retrieve the Eye of Horus."

They spent the next few hours preparing for their respective journeys. We gathered supplies, studied maps, and exchanged farewells. Neferet felt a mixture of anxiety and determination as she prepared to leave. The fate of her kingdom rested on their success.

As the sun set, casting a fiery glow over the horizon, Neferet and Amara set out for the Valley of the Kings. The journey was fraught with danger, but Neferet's resolve was unwavering. She knew the path ahead would be difficult, but she was determined to save her people and break the curse.

The Valley of the Kings was a place of ancient power and mystery. As they approached, Neferet felt a sense of awe and reverence. The tombs of Pharaohs and nobles lay hidden beneath the rocky landscape, their secrets guarded by the spirits of the past.

"We need to find the Sacred Lotus," Neferet said, her eyes scanning the area. "The scroll mentioned a hidden oasis where it blooms."

They searched for hours, following the clues provided by the ancient texts. Finally, they came upon a secluded oasis, its waters sparkling under the moonlight. In the center of the oasis, a single lotus flower glowed with an ethereal light.

Neferet approached the flower, feeling a sense of reverence. "This is it. The Sacred Lotus."

As she reached out to pluck the flower, a sudden movement caught her eye. From the shadows emerged a group of spectral guardians, their forms shimmering with otherworldly energy. They moved to protect the lotus, their eyes filled with an ancient, unwavering duty.

Neferet stepped forward, her voice calm but firm. "We mean no harm. We seek to end the curse that plagues our land. Please, allow us to take the lotus."

The guardians hesitated, their forms wavering. One of them stepped forward, its voice echoing in Neferet's mind. "The curse is a blight upon the land. If you seek to end it, you may take the lotus. But beware, peril awaits along the path ahead."

Neferet nodded, her resolve unwavering. "Thank you. We will face whatever challenges come our way."

With great care, she plucked the Sacred Lotus and placed it in a protective pouch. As they made their way back to the palace, Neferet felt a renewed sense of hope. They had taken the first step in their quest to break the curse.

Upon their return, the other teams greeted Neferet and Amara with news. Anen and Paser had successfully retrieved the Scepter of Ra from the Temple of Karnak, and Khepri's team had secured the Eye of Horus from the nomadic tribe.

With all the artifacts in their possession, Neferet knew the time performed the ritual. They held the fate of the kingdom in their hands, and she was determined to succeed. The final confrontation with Seti was imminent, and Neferet was ready to face the darkness and bring peace to her land.

Chapter 5

Secrets of the Pharaoh's Court

The sun rose over Thebes, casting a warm glow on the palace as Neferet, Anen, Paser, Amara, and Khepri gathered in the royal chamber. The sacred artifacts—the Amulet of Seti, the Scepter of Ra, the Sacred Lotus, and the Eye of Horus—lay before them, their combined presence filling the room with an aura of ancient power.

"We have all the artifacts," Neferet said, her voice filled with determination. "Now we must understand how to use them to break the curse."

Anen nodded, his wise eyes scanning the scrolls spread out on the table. "The scrolls provide some clues, but they are fragmented."" We need to piece together the ritual steps and ensure we understand each element."

Paser, the head scribe, carefully examined the hieroglyphs on the scrolls. "These symbols show a connection between the artifacts and the elements—earth, water, fire, and air. Each artifact represents one of these elements and the user must use them in harmony to break the curse."

Neferet looked at the artifacts, her mind racing. "The Sacred Lotus represents water, the Eye of Horus symbolizes air, the Scepter of Ra embodies fire, and the Amulet of Seti is linked to earth. We must perform the ritual at a place where these elements converge."

Khepri stepped forward, his expression thoughtful. Many people say that the Great Pyramid of Giza serves as a focal point of elemental power. Many people believe that earth, water, fire, and air intersect at this place.

"Then we must travel to Giza," Neferet declared. "We will perform the ritual there and put an end to this curse."

As they prepared for the journey, Neferet sought her father, Pharaoh Ramses, to inform him of their plan. She found him in his private chambers, studying a map of the kingdom.

"Father," Neferet said, bowing respectfully. "We have discovered how to break the curse. We must travel to the Great Pyramid of Giza and perform an ancient ritual using the artifacts we have gathered."

Pharaoh Ramses looked at his daughter, pride and concern clear in his eyes. "You have shown great courage and wisdom, Neferet. I believe in you. May the gods watch over you and guide you on this perilous journey."

Neferet embraced her father, feeling his strength and support bolstering her resolve. "Thank you, Father. I will not fail."

Neferet and her companions were determined during the long and arduous journey to Giza. They traveled by boat along the Nile, then continued on foot through the desert. Along the way, they encountered challenges and dangers, but their combined skills and unwavering determination saw them through.

As they approached the Great Pyramid, its imposing silhouette rising against the sky, Neferet felt a sense of awe and trepidation. The pyramid was a symbol of ancient power and mystery, and it was here that they would face their greatest challenge.

They set up camp near the base of the pyramid, and Anen prepared the ritual space. He drew a large circle in the sand, marking it with symbols and placing the artifacts at the cardinal points.

"We must perform the ritual at sunrise," Anen explained. "The first light of dawn will amplify the elemental energies and help us break the curse."

As they waited for dawn, Neferet and her companions reviewed their roles in the ritual. Each of them would need to channel the power of an artifact and recite an incantation in unison.

The night passed slowly, and the tension in the air was palpable. As the first rays of the sun peeked over the horizon, they took their positions within the circle.

Neferet held the Amulet of Seti, representing Earth. Anen took the Scepter of Ra, symbolizing fire. Paser held the Sacred Lotus, embodying water. Khepri held the Eye of Horus, representing the air. Amara stood beside Neferet, ready to provide support and strength.

As the sun rose, they chanted the incantation, their voices blending harmoniously. The artifacts glowed with an ethereal light, and the elemental energies surged around them. The ground trembled, and a powerful wind swept through the desert, swirling around the pyramid.

Seti's spectral form appeared above the pyramid, his eyes burning with rage and defiance. "You cannot break the curse!" he bellowed. "My power is eternal!"

Neferet's voice rang out, strong and unwavering. "We will break the curse, Seti. Your reign of terror ends today!"

The light from the artifacts intensified, converging into a brilliant beam that pierced the sky. Seti's form wavered, and he let out a scream of fury as the light enveloped him.

"Now!" Anen shouted. "Channel all your energy into the ritual!"

Neferet focused all her willpower on the amulet, feeling its ancient power flow through her. The beam of light grew even brighter, and Seti's form disintegrated, his screams fading into the wind.

With a final burst of energy, the light exploded in a dazzling display, and Seti's presence vanished. The ground stopped trembling, and the wind died down, leaving an eerie silence in its wake.

Neferet and her companions stood in the circle, their breaths coming in ragged gasps. The artifacts lay quiet despite that, their power spent.

"It's over, "Neferet said, her voice filled with relief. "We have broken the curse."

As the sun rose fully over the horizon, bathing the desert in golden light, Neferet felt a profound sense of peace. They had faced the darkness and emerged victorious. The kingdom was safe, and its curse that had plagued her bloodline for generations was finally lifted.

They made their way back to the palace together and found joyous celebrations awaiting them. The people of Thebes hailed Neferet as a hero, and her bravery and determination became the stuff of legend.

Pharaoh Ramses embraced his daughter, his eyes shining with pride. "You have done it, Neferet. You have saved our kingdom."

Neferet smiled, feeling a deep sense of fulfillment. "We did it together, Father. With the help of our allies and the strength of our ancestors, we have ensured that the light of our kingdom will shine for generations to come."

And so, with the curse lifted and peace restored, Neferet's story became a beacon of hope and inspiration, a testament to the power of courage, wisdom, and unity in the face of darkness.

Chapter 6

The Princess's Quest Begins

The celebrations in Thebes were grand and filled with joy, but Neferet knew their journey was far from over. The curse may have been temporarily subdued, but the dark forces that Seti had unleashed were still a threat. Researchers gathered the artifacts and performed the ritual, but they still had many unanswered questions. Neferet realized that to ensure lasting peace for her kingdom, she needed to seek more knowledge and understanding of the ancient powers they had confronted.

Neferet convened a meeting with her closest allies in the royal chamber. Anen, Paser, Amara, and Khepri all gathered around the large wooden table, their faces reflecting a mix of relief and determination.

"We have won," Neferet began, her voice steady and resolute. "But our quest is not yet complete. We need to understand more about the ancient magic and the true extent of Seti's curse to ensure it never threatens our kingdom again."

Anen nodded in agreement. "Indeed, Princess. The ritual we performed was only a temporary measure. To secure lasting peace, we must seek the source of Seti's power and destroy it completely."

Paser, ever the scholar, laid out a series of ancient maps and scrolls on the table. "Legends tell of a hidden library deep within the desert, where they keep the secrets of the ancients. Powerful beings guard it and intricate traps protect it. If we can find this library, we might uncover the knowledge we need."

Amara looked at Neferet with concern. "The journey will be dangerous, Neferet. Are you sure we should risk it?"

Neferet met Amara's gaze with determination. "We have faced many dangers already, and we have overcome them together. We must continue to be brave and strong. For the sake of our people, we cannot shy away from this challenge."

Khepri, the warrior, spoke up. "I will lead a team to scout ahead and ensure the path is safe. We will face any dangers head-on and protect you, Princess."

With their plan set, Neferet and her companions prepared for the journey. We gathered supplies and made the preparations. As they set out from Thebes, the people of the kingdom lined the streets to bid them farewell, their faces filled with hope and gratitude.

The journey through the desert was grueling. The sun beat down mercilessly, and the sands shifted unpredictably under their feet. Despite the harsh conditions, Neferet and her companions pressed on, their spirits unwavering. They encountered various challenges along the way—sandstorms that obscured their path, treacherous terrain that tested their endurance, and wild creatures that threatened their safety.

One night, as they made camp under the starlit sky, Neferet sat by the fire, deep in thought. Amara joined her, her expression filled with concern.

"Neferet, do you ever doubt our mission?" Amara asked softly.

Neferet looked at her friend, her eyes reflecting the firelight. "I would be lying if I said I didn't have moments of doubt, Amara. But I know we are doing what is right. We must uncover the truth and protect our people. That gives me strength."

Amara smiled, her worry easing slightly. "You have always been strong and determined, Neferet. I believe in you."

As dawn broke, they continued their journey, following the ancient maps and the guidance of the stars. After many days of travel, they arrived at the entrance to a hidden valley surrounded by towering cliffs and guarded by statues of ancient gods.

"This must be the place," Paser said, his voice filled with awe. "The hidden library lies within this valley."

They carefully made their way into the valley, their senses heightened and their movements cautious. The air was thick with an otherworldly presence, and the statues seemed to watch them with silent vigilance. As they ventured deeper, they encountered a series of puzzles and traps designed to protect the library from intruders.

Working together, they deciphered the ancient symbols and navigated the treacherous pathways. Each challenge they faced required a combination of their skills—Neferet's leadership, Anen's wisdom, Paser's knowledge, Khepri's strength, and Amara's agility.

Finally, they reached the entrance to the hidden library, a grand doorway adorned with intricate carvings and glowing with a faint, mystical light. Pushing open the heavy doors, they encountered a sight that left them breathless.

The library was vast, its walls lined with shelves that reached up to the high ceiling, filled with scrolls and tablets containing the wisdom of ages. The scent of ancient parchment and the faint hum of magical energy filled the air.

Neferet stepped forward, her heart pounding with excitement and reverence. "This is it. The knowledge we seek is here."

They spread out, each of them searching the shelves and studying the scrolls. By delving into the ancient texts, they uncovered secrets and insights that time had lost, and days passed quickly.

One evening, as Neferet pored over an old and fragile scroll, she discovered a passage that sent a chill down her spine. It spoke of a dark relic, a source of immense power that Seti had used to fuel his dark magic. Powerful spirits guarded the relic, known as the Eye of Set, deep within the underworld, and deadly traps protected it.

"We must find and destroy the Eye of Set," Neferet declared, her voice filled with resolve. "It is the source of Seti's power, and if we can destroy it, we can ensure that his curse will never return."

The journey to the underworld would be their greatest challenge yet, but Neferet and her companions were ready. With the knowledge they had gained from the hidden library, they had the tools and the understanding they needed to confront the darkness head-on.

As they left the hidden library and prepared for the next leg of their quest, Neferet felt a deep sense of purpose and determination. They had come so far and faced so many dangers, but the end was in sight. Together, they would overcome the final obstacles and secure the lasting peace and safety of their kingdom.

Their journey had only just begun, and Neferet knew that the trials ahead would be the most difficult yet. But with her loyal friends by her side and the wisdom of the ancients guiding her, she was ready to face whatever challenges lay ahead and fulfill her destiny as the protector of her people.

Chapter 7

The Enigmatic Sphinx

The hidden library had provided Neferet and her companions with invaluable knowledge about Seti and the Eye of Set. Armed with this newfound understanding, they set out on the next leg of their journey to seek the guidance of the Sphinx. The Sphinx was an ancient guardian known for its wisdom and riddles, said to hold crucial knowledge about the curse and the path to the underworld.

The journey to the Sphinx was arduous, taking them through barren deserts and treacherous mountain passes. Each step brought them closer to their goal, but the harsh environment tested their endurance and resolve. Despite the difficulties, Neferet's determination never wavered. She knew the Sphinx held the key to uncovering the final pieces of their quest.

After days of travel, they arrived at the base of a towering cliff. At the top stood the Sphinx, its massive stone form carved with intricate details and symbols that seemed to pulse with ancient power. The Sphinx's eyes, though made of stone, seemed to gaze down upon them with a knowing intensity.

Neferet approached the Sphinx, her heart pounding with anticipation. "Great Sphinx," she called out, her voice echoing against the cliffs. "We seek your wisdom and guidance. We must break the curse of Seti and destroy the Eye of Set. Please, reveal to us the path we must take."

The ground beneath them trembled, and a deep, resonant voice emanated from the Sphinx. "Those who seek my wisdom must prove themselves worthy. Answer my riddle, and I shall grant you the knowledge you seek. "If you fail, we will turn you away.""

Neferet nodded, steeling herself for the challenge. "We are ready. Please, ask your riddle."

The Sphinx's eyes glowed with a faint light as it spoke. "I am not alive, but I can grow. I don't have lungs, but I need air. I don't have a mouth, but water kills me. What am I?"

Neferet's mind raced as she considered the riddle. Those who sought the Sphinx's guidance knew its riddles were challenging, designed to test wisdom and intellect. She thought of the clues: something that grows, needs air, and water kills.

After a moment of contemplation, Neferet's eyes widened with realization. "Fire," she said confidently. "The answer is fire."

The Sphinx was silent for a moment before its eyes glowed brighter, and the ground ceased to tremble. "You have answered correctly," it intoned. "You have proven your worthiness. Now, I shall reveal to you the knowledge you seek."

The Sphinx's eyes projected a beam of light that formed a map in the air before them. The map unveiled a concealed path that extended deep into the underworld, revealing the hiding place of the Eye of Set. It also showed the locations of the guardians and traps that protected the relic.

"The path to the underworld is fraught with peril," the Sphinx warned. "You will face many trials and challenges. But with courage and wisdom, you can succeed. To break the curse forever, we must destroy the Eye of Set."

Neferet and her companions studied the map, committing its details to memory. They knew that the journey ahead would be their most dangerous yet, but they were ready to face whatever challenges lay ahead.

"Thank you, great Sphinx," Neferet said, bowing respectfully. "We will honor your wisdom and use it to save our kingdom."

As they made their way back down the cliff, the weight of their task settled upon them. They had the knowledge they needed, but the journey to the underworld would test their limits. Neferet felt a mixture of fear and determination, knowing that the fate of her kingdom rested on their success.

That night, they camped at the base of the cliff, preparing for the journey ahead. Neferet sat by the fire. The map of the underworld spread out before her. Amara joined her, her expression filled with concern.

"Neferet, are you sure we're ready for this?" Amara asked softly. "The underworld is a place of great danger."

Neferet looked at her friend, her eyes filled with determination. "I know it will be dangerous, Amara. But we have come so far and faced so much already. We cannot turn back now. The future of our kingdom depends on us."

Amara nodded, her worry easing slightly. "I believe in you, Neferet. And I will stand by your side, no matter what."

The next morning, they set out for the entrance to the underworld, following the map provided by the Sphinx. The path led them to a secluded cave, its entrance shrouded in darkness and marked by ancient symbols.

"This is it," Paser said, his voice filled with awe. "The entrance to the underworld."

Neferet took a deep breath, steeling herself for the challenges ahead. "We will face whatever lies within and emerge victorious. For our people, for our kingdom."

As they stepped into the cave, the darkness enveloped them, and the air grew heavy with an otherworldly presence. They knew their journey had only just begun, and the trials of the underworld awaited them. But with the knowledge of the Sphinx and their unwavering determination, they were ready to face whatever challenges lay ahead and secure the future of their kingdom.

Chapter 8

The Curse Unleashed

The cave's entrance closed behind them, sealing Neferet and her companions in complete darkness. The air was thick and heavy, filled with the scent of ancient stone and the faint whispers of the underworld. Neferet held her torch high, its flickering light casting eerie shadows on the walls as they moved deeper into the cave.

They followed the map provided by the Sphinx, their path illuminated only by the dim glow of their torches. The silence was oppressive, broken only by the sound of their footsteps and the occasional distant rumble. Every step they took seemed to echo through the caverns, amplifying their sense of isolation.

"We must stay vigilant," Anen warned, his voice a hushed whisper. "Traps and guardians fill the underworld. We must prepare for anything."

Neferet nodded, her grip tightening on the amulet of Seti. "We will face whatever comes our way. We must reach the Eye of Set and destroy it."

As they ventured further, the temperature dropped, and a cold, clammy mist filled the air. Strange, ghostly figures flickered in and out of the mist, their forms barely visible but deeply unsettling. Neferet felt a chill run down her spine, but she forced herself to remain focused.

After hours of navigating the twisting tunnels, they arrived at a massive stone door covered in intricate carvings and ancient symbols. The door seemed to pulsate with dark energy, and Neferet could feel the malevolent power emanating from it.

"This is it," Khepri said, his voice steady. "The first of many trials."

Neferet stepped forward, examining the symbols on the door. They matched those on the amulet, showing that the amulet was the key to unlocking the door. She carefully placed the amulet into a recess, and with a deep rumble, the door opened.

Beyond the door lay a vast chamber filled with towering statues of ancient gods and a series of stone platforms suspended over a bottomless chasm. Narrow, precarious bridges connected the platforms, and the air was thick with the sound of whispering voices.

"We must cross the platforms," Neferet said, her voice resolute. "But we must be careful. One wrong step, and we could fall."

They moved cautiously, balancing on the narrow bridges as they made their way across the chasm. The whispering voices grew louder, filling their minds with doubt and fear. Neferet felt the weight of the whispers pressing down on her, but she pushed forward, determined to reach the other side.

Halfway across, the ground beneath them shook, and the platforms started to shift and crumble. A dark, shadowy figure emerged from the chasm, its eyes glowing with an unholy light. It was one guardian of the underworld, a creature of immense power and malice.

"Hold on!" Khepri shouted, drawing his sword. "We must fight our way through!"

The guardian lunged at them, its claws slashing through the air. Khepri and Amara moved to intercept it, their weapons clashing with the creature's dark energy. Neferet focused on keeping her balance, guiding Paser and Anen across the crumbling platforms.

As the battle raged, Neferet felt a surge of energy from the amulet. She raised it high, channeling its power to create a barrier of light that pushed the guardian back. The creature howled in pain, its form flickering and weakening.

"Now!" Neferet shouted. "We must cross now!"

With renewed determination, they sprinted across the remaining platforms, barely making it to the other side as the chasm collapsed behind them. The guardian's howls faded into the distance, and the chamber fell silent once more.

"We did it," Paser said, panting. "But we must keep moving. The worst is yet to come."

They continued through the underworld, facing a series of increasingly difficult trials. In each chamber, adventurers faced new challenges, such as crossing fiery pits, solving riddles, and defeating spectral guardians. With each trial, Neferet's resolve grew stronger, and the bond between her and her companions deepened.

Finally, they reached the heart of the underworld, a massive cavern filled with dark, swirling energy. At the center of the cavern stood a pedestal upon which rested the Eye of Set. The relic pulsed with a malevolent light, and the surrounding air crackled with dark magic.

"This is it," Neferet said, her voice filled with determination. "The source of Seti's power."

As they approached the pedestal, the ground shook violently, and a dark figure emerged from the shadows. It was Seti, his spectral form more powerful and terrifying than ever.

"You dare to challenge me?" Seti's voice echoed through the cavern, filled with rage and contempt. "You are fools to think you can destroy my power."

Neferet stepped forward, her eyes blazing with determination. "We will stop you, Seti. Your reign of terror ends here."

Seti laughed, a chilling sound that reverberated through the cavern. "You are no match for me. The power of the Eye of Set is beyond your comprehension."

The battle that ensued was fierce and desperate. Seti summoned dark spirits and unleashed waves of dark energy, but Neferet and her companions fought with all their might. Khepri's sword clashed with Seti's dark magic, Amara's agility allowed her to evade the spirits, and Anen and Paser used their knowledge to weaken Seti's defenses.

Neferet focused all her energy on the amulet, channeling its power into a beam of light that struck the Eye of Set. The relic pulsed and crackled, its dark energy beginning to waver.

"You cannot defeat me!" Seti roared, his form flickering with rage. "The curse is eternal!"

With a final, desperate effort, Neferet poured all her strength into the amulet. The beam of light intensified, piercing through the Eye of Set and shattering it into a million fragments. Seti let out a final, agonized scream as his form disintegrated, his dark power vanquished forever.

The cavern fell silent, the dark energy dissipating into nothingness. Neferet and her companions stood victorious, their breaths coming in ragged gasps. The curse broke and destroyed the Eye of Set.

"We did it," Neferet said, her voice filled with relief and triumph. "The curse is finally broken."

As they made their way back to the surface, Neferet felt a profound sense of peace. They had faced the darkness and emerged victorious. The kingdom of Thebes was safe, and the legacy of Seti's curse was finally laid to rest.

Joyous celebrations greeted them as they returned to the palace. The people of Thebes hailed Neferet and her companions as heroes, their bravery and determination becoming the stuff of legend.

Pharaoh Ramses embraced his daughter, his eyes filled with pride and gratitude. "You have done it, Neferet. You have saved our kingdom."

Neferet smiled, feeling a deep sense of fulfillment. "We did it together, Father. With the help of our allies and the strength of our ancestors, we have ensured that the light of our kingdom will shine for generations to come."

And so, with the curse lifted and peace restored, Neferet's story became a beacon of hope and inspiration, a testament to the power of courage, wisdom, and unity in the face of darkness. Generations would tell the adventures of Neferet and her companions, reminding us of the strength and resilience of the human spirit.

Chapter 9

Trials of the Underworld

The journey through the underworld had been a harrowing experience, but Neferet and her companions knew that the true trial still lay ahead. The knowledge they had gained and the artifacts they had gathered were crucial, but the final test would require all their courage, wisdom, and strength. They had faced Seti and destroyed the Eye of Set, but the underworld held more challenges before they could return to the surface and secure lasting peace for their kingdom.

As they descended deeper into the underworld, the air grew colder, and the surrounding darkness seemed to thicken. The path ahead was treacherous, filled with obstacles and traps designed to test their resolve.

"Stay close," Neferet instructed, her voice steady despite the unease gnawing at her. "We must remain vigilant."

They entered a vast cavern filled with towering stone pillars and deep chasms. The only way forward was across a series of narrow, precarious bridges suspended over the abyss. An eerie, almost tangible tension filled the air.

"We must cross carefully," Khepri said, eyeing the bridges warily. "One misstep could be fatal."

Neferet led the way, her steps deliberate and cautious. As they crossed the first bridge, a sudden gust of wind swept through the cavern, causing the bridge to sway dangerously. Neferet gripped the rope railings tightly, urging her companions to do the same.

"Keep moving!" she called out. "We can't afford to stop now."

One by one, they made their way across the bridges, each step a test of their balance and nerve. The wind howled around them, and the chasms below seemed to whisper with malevolent intent. Despite the danger, they pressed on, their determination unshaken.

As they reached the final bridge, a dark figure emerged from the shadows, blocking their path. It was one of the ancient guardians of the underworld, its form shrouded in darkness and its eyes glowing with an otherworldly light.

"To pass, you must face me," the guardian intoned, its voice echoing through the cavern. "Prove your worth, or the abyss will condemn you."

Khepri stepped forward, his sword drawn. "We will face you," he declared. "We will prove our worth."

The guardian lunged at Khepri. Its movements were swift and deadly. Khepri met its attack with a clash of steel, his strength and skill on full display. The battle was intense, the guardian's dark power pushing Khepri to his limits. But Khepri fought with unwavering resolve, his every move calculated and precise.

As Khepri battled the guardian, Neferet noticed that the amulet she carried glowed faintly. Realizing that the amulet's power could aid them, she raised it high, focusing its energy on the guardian. A beam of light shot forth, striking the guardian and weakening its dark form.

"Now, Khepri!" Neferet shouted. "Strike now!"

With a final, powerful blow, Khepri defeated the guardian, its dark form dissipating into the shadows. The path ahead was clear, and they quickly crossed the final bridge, reaching the other side safely.

"We're almost there," Neferet said, her voice filled with determination. "The trials are not over yet, but we will succeed."

They entered the next chamber and found it filled with a dense, choking mist. The air was heavy with the scent of decay, and strange, ghostly figures moved through the mist, their eyes empty and lifeless.

"We must navigate this mist," Anen said, his voice calm but urgent. "Stay close and do not stray from the path."

They moved carefully through the mist, each step feeling like a struggle against an unseen force. The ghostly figures reached out to them, their touch cold and draining. Neferet felt a wave of despair wash over her, but she pushed forward, her resolve unyielding.

"Focus on the light," she urged her companions. "Do not let the darkness take hold."

With great effort, they made their way through the mist, emerging into a chamber bathed in an eerie blue light. At the center of the chamber stood a pedestal, upon which rested a glowing crystal. The crystal pulsed with a rhythmic light, and Neferet felt a strange connection to it.

"This is the Heart of the Underworld," Anen explained. "It is said to hold the power of the ancients. We must harness its energy to complete our journey."

Neferet approached the crystal, her hand outstretched. As she touched it, a surge of energy flowed through her, filling her with strength and clarity. The crystal light intensified, illuminating the chamber and dispelling the lingering darkness.

"We have the power we need," Neferet said, her voice strong. "Let's move forward."

With the Heart of the Underworld's power guiding them, they continued their journey. The final chamber they entered was vast and filled with a sense of ancient, overwhelming power. At its center stood a grand altar, surrounded by statues of long-forgotten gods.

"This is the final trial," Paser said, his voice filled with reverence. "We must perform a ritual to seal the underworld and ensure that Seti's curse never returns."

Neferet and her companions took their places around the altar, each holding the artifact they had gathered. They chanted the incantation Anen had taught them, their voices blending harmoniously and resonating through the chamber.

As they chanted, the artifacts glowed, their combined light forming a powerful, protective barrier. The ground trembled, and a dark, swirling vortex appeared above the altar, filled with the remnants of Seti's dark energy.

"Focus your energy on the artifacts!" Neferet instructed. "We must seal the vortex!"

With all their strength and determination, they channeled their energy into the artifacts. The light grew brighter, and the vortex shrank, its dark energy dissipating into nothingness.

Finally, with a blinding flash of light, the vortex closed, and the chamber fell silent. The ground ceased to tremble, and the oppressive darkness lifted, replaced by a sense of peace and tranquility.

"We did it," Neferet said, her voice filled with relief and triumph. "The trials are over. Someone has broken the curse."

As they made their way back to the surface, Neferet felt a profound sense of accomplishment. They'd had faced the trials of the underworld and emerged victorious. The kingdom of Thebes remained safe, and they put Seti's curse to rest.

Joyous celebrations greeted them when they returned to the palace. The people of Thebes hailed Neferet and her companions as heroes, their bravery and determination becoming the stuff of legend.

Pharaoh Ramses embraced his daughter, his eyes filled with pride and gratitude. "You have done it, Neferet. You have saved our kingdom."

Neferet smiled, feeling a deep sense of fulfillment. "We did it together, Father. With the help of our allies and the strength of our ancestors, we have ensured that the light of our kingdom will shine for generations to come."

And so, with the trials of the underworld behind them and peace restored, Neferet's story became a beacon of hope and inspiration, a testament to the power of courage, wisdom, and unity in the face of darkness. Future generations will tell the adventures of Neferet and her companions as a reminder of the strength and resilience of the human spirit.

Chapter 10

The Final Confrontation and Redemption

Neferet knew she had saved the kingdom of Thebes from the immediate threat of Seti's curse, but the true test was yet to come. The underworld had revealed the depths of the curse's power, and while they had successfully sealed the dark vortex, Seti's presence still loomed over them. Neferet awaited the final confrontation with the mummy himself and was determined to end his reign of terror once and for all.

Neferet gathered her closest allies in the royal chamber as they made preparations for the final battle. Anen, Paser, Amara, and Khepri stood by her side, their faces resolute.

"We have come a long way," Neferet began, her voice steady. "We have faced countless challenges and overcome them together. Now we must confront Seti himself.,"We must be prepared for anything because this is our final battle.""

Anen stepped forward, holding the ancient scrolls that had guided them thus far. "The ritual we performed has weakened Seti, but he is still a formidable foe. We must use the artifacts and our combined strength to defeat him once and for all."

Paser, ever the scholar, added, "The final battle must take place in the Valley of the Kings, where Seti's tomb lies. It is there that his power is strongest, and it is there that we must confront him."

Khepri, the warrior, clenched his fist. "We will face him and end this curse. For the sake of our kingdom and our people, we cannot fail."

With their plan set, Neferet and her companions prepared for the journey to the Valley of the Kings. The people of Thebes gathered to see them off, their faces filled with hope and gratitude. As they departed, Neferet felt a sense of calm determination. She knew that this was the moment she had been preparing for her entire life.

The Valley of the Kings was a place of ancient power and mystery, its rocky landscape dotted with the tombs of pharaohs and nobles. As they approached Seti's tomb, the air grew heavy with a sense of foreboding. Towering statues of ancient gods marked the entrance to the tomb, their eyes watching their every move.

"This is it," Neferet said, her voice filled with resolve. "The final confrontation."

As they entered the tomb, the darkness closed in around them, and the air grew colder. Intricate carvings lined the walls, depicting Seti's rise to power and his eventual fall. At the end of the corridor, they reached a large chamber, its ceiling supported by massive stone columns. At the center of the chamber lay Seti's sarcophagus, its surface covered in glowing hieroglyphs.

Suddenly, the air crackled with dark energy, and Seti's spectral form emerged from the sarcophagus. His eyes burned with rage and malevolence, and his presence filled the chamber with an overwhelming sense of dread.

"You dare to challenge me?" Seti's voice echoed through the chamber, filled with contempt. "You are fools to think you can defeat me."

Neferet stepped forward, her eyes blazing with determination. "We will stop you, Seti. Your reign of terror ends here."

Seti laughed, a chilling sound that reverberated through the chamber. "You are no match for me. My power is eternal."

The battle that ensued was fierce and desperate. Seti summoned dark spirits and unleashed waves of dark energy, but Neferet and her companions fought with all their might. Khepri's sword clashed with Seti's dark magic, Amara's agility allowed her to evade the spirits, and Anen and Paser used their knowledge to weaken Seti's defenses.

Neferet focused all her energy on the amulet, channeling its power into a beam of light that struck Seti. The relics they had gathered glowed, their combined light forming a powerful barrier against Seti's dark energy.

"You cannot defeat me!" Seti roared, his form flickering with rage. "The curse is eternal!"

With a final, desperate effort, Neferet poured all her strength into the amulet. The beam of light intensified, piercing through Seti and shattering his form. As the light consumed his spirit, Seti let out a final, agonized scream, vanquishing his dark power forever.

The chamber fell silent, the dark energy dissipating into nothingness. Neferet and her companions stood victorious, their breaths coming in ragged gasps. Seti finally eradicated his presence by breaking the curse.

"We did it," Neferet said, her voice filled with relief and triumph. "We broke the curse."

As they made their way back to the surface, the weight of their task lifted from their shoulders. The kingdom of Thebes was safe, and the legacy of Seti's curse was finally laid to rest. Upon their return to the palace, joyful celebrations greeted them. The people of Thebes hailed Neferet and her companions as heroes, their bravery and determination becoming the stuff of legend. Greeted with joyous celebrations. The people of Thebes hailed Neferet and her companions as heroes, their bravery and determination becoming the stuff of legend.

Pharaoh Ramses embraced his daughter, his eyes filled with pride and gratitude. "You have done it, Neferet. You have saved our kingdom."

Neferet smiled, feeling a deep sense of fulfillment. "We did it together, Father. With the help of our allies and the strength of our ancestors, we have ensured that the light of our kingdom will shine for generations to come."

The celebrations continued long into the night, with music, dancing, and feasting. Neferet felt a profound sense of peace and contentment, knowing that they had secured the future of their kingdom.

As the sun rose the next morning, casting a golden glow over the palace, Neferet stood on the balcony, looking out over the city. She knew that there would always be challenges ahead, but she felt ready to face them with courage and wisdom.

The story of Neferet and her companions became a beacon of hope and inspiration, a testament to the power of courage, wisdom, and unity in the face of darkness. Generations told their adventures, reminding others of the strength and resilience of the human spirit.

And so, as people stood together and faced their challenges with unwavering resolve, they lifted the curse, restored peace, and kept Neferet's legacy alive as a shining example of what they could achieve. The light of Thebes shone brightly, a symbol of hope and prosperity for all who called it home.